For Anna and Charlotte, with love...xx ~ TC

For Matthew C, Dave T, and Andy B, hands-on super dads!
And to all new parents – good luck... ~ TW

tiger tales

5 River Road, Suite 128, Wilton, CT 06897
Published in the United States 2013
Originally published in Great Britain 2013
by Little Tiger Press
Text copyright © 2013 Tracey Corderoy
Illustrations copyright © 2013 Tim Warnes
CIP data is available
ISBN-13: 978-1-58925-150-2
ISBN-10: 1-58925-150-4
Printed in China
LTP/1400/0569/0313

For more insight and activities,
visit us at www.tigertalesbooks.com

by Tracey Corderoy

Illustrated by Tim Warnes

tiger tales

Otto was adorable.
Everybody said so.

Adorable dimples!

Then Otto learned a brand-new word . . .

Otto *loved* his new word. So he said it more and more.

He said it at mealtimes.

He said it at bath times.

And he said it at every single bedtime.

When it was time to go out, Otto got himself ready.

But would he put his coat on?

Otto practiced his new favorite word at school.

Can we play dinosaurs, Otto?

No!

Unfortunately, that didn't go so well.

Soon, Otto was saying his word all the time. But sometimes he wished he hadn't.

Come and join our train, Otto.

No!

Hey, where'd everybody go?

As time went on, his little word became a big, **big** problem.

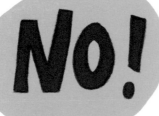

When it was time to go home, Daddy asked, "Did you have a nice day?" Otto gave a little sniff.

"Would you like a hug?"
"N-nnnnn . . ."

WAAAH!

Now Otto has a
new favorite word . . .

Hey, Otto!
Do you want
to play?